FIRST FLIGHT®

*FIRST FLIGHT® is an exciting new series
of beginning readers.
The series presents titles which include songs,
poems, adventures, mysteries, and humor
by established authors and illustrators.
FIRST FLIGHT® makes the introduction to reading fun
and satisfying for the young reader.*

*FIRST FLIGHT® is available in 4 levels
to correspond to reading development.*

Level 1 – Preschool - Grade 1
Large type, repetition of simple concepts that are perfect for reading aloud, easy vocabulary and endearing characters in short simple stories for the earliest reader.

Level 2 – Grade 1 - Grade 3
Longer sentences, higher level of vocabulary, repetition, and high-interest stories for the progressing reader.

Level 3 – Grade 2 - Grade 4
Simple stories with more involved plots and a simple chapter format for the newly independent reader.

Level 4 – Grade 3 - up (First Flight Chapter Books)
More challenging level, minimal illustrations for the independent reader.

First four books in the First Flight® series

Level 1 • **Fishes in the Ocean** *written by* Maggee Spicer *and* Richard Thompson, *illustrated by* Barbara Hartmann

Level 2 • **Jingle Bells** *written and illustrated by* Maryann Kovalski

Level 3 • **Andrew's Magnificent Mountain of Mittens** *written by* Deanne Lee Bingham, *illustrated by* Kim LaFave

Level 4 • **The Money Boot** *written by* Ginny Russell, *illustrated by* John Mardon

To Misha and Hally Starr
Two sweet sisters and two great travellers.

FIRST FLIGHT® is a registered trademark of Fitzhenry and Whiteside

Jingle Bells
Copyright © 1998 by Maryann Kovalski

First publication in the United States in 1999.

Fitzhenry & Whiteside acknowledges with thanks the support of the Government of Canada through its Book Publishing Industry Development Program in the publication of this title.

Design by Wycliffe Smith.

Printed in Canada.

10 9 8 7 6 5 4 3 2 1

Canadian Cataloguing in Publication Data

Kovalski, Maryann
Jingle bells

(A first flight reader)
ISBN 1-55041-393-7 (bound)
ISBN 1-55041-383-X (pbk.)

I. Title. II. Series.

PS8571.O96J55 1998   jC813'.54   C98-931542-8
PZ8.3.K8535 Ji 1998

A First Flight® Level Two Reader

Maryann Kovalski

Fitzhenry and Whiteside • Toronto

"Wake up, Jenny,"
said Joanna.

"No," said Jenny,
"I am tired."

"But today is a special day,"
said Joanna,
"Grandma is coming!

We will take a taxi.
We will take a plane.
We will stay in a big hotel."

"No," said Jenny,
"It is not today.
It is tomorrow."

Jenny pulled the covers
over her head.
"Go back to bed."

"Oh," said Joanna,
"I have made a mistake."

Joanna got back into bed.
She pulled the covers
over her head.

Jenny jumped up.
She was all dressed.

"Ha!" said Jenny,
"I tricked you!"

"You must hurry, Joanna!"
said Jenny,

"Grandma will soon
be here."

Joanna dressed quickly.

Grandma arrived.

They took a taxi to the airport.

"I hope we did not forget anything." said Jenny.

"I hope we did not forget anything." said Joanna.

"Oh, I do hope we did not forget anything," said Grandma.

"I do not think that you forgot anything," said the man who carried the bags.

The plane was fun.
They got crayons.

They got juice.
They got up and down.

They took a taxi to the hotel.
The hotel was big.
It had a lot of flags.

People on the street were
in a hurry.
There was a lot of noise.

A man on the sidewalk was singing.
People put coins in his box.
The coins made
a jingle sound.

A jolly Santa
stood on the corner.
He was ringing a bell.
The bell made
a jingle sound.

A lady on the street waved her arm.
She was calling a taxi.
The bracelets she wore
made a jingle sound.

A horse and carriage
sped along the street.
The horse had bells
on his harness.
The bells made
a jingle sound.

"All those jingle sounds
have given me an idea,"
said Grandma.
"Let's sing!"

Jingle bells! Jingle bells!
Jingle all the way!
Oh, what fun it is to ride
On a one-horse open sleigh!

Dashing through the snow
On a one-horse open sleigh,

O'er the fields we cross,
Laughing all the way!
Ho, Ho, Ho,

Bells on bobtails ring,
Making spirits bright!
Oh, what fun it is to sing
A sleighing song tonight!

Jingle Bells, Jingle Bells!
Jingle all the way!

What fun it is to ride

on a one horse open sleigh!

Jenny, Joanna and Grandma
had so much fun
singing that . . .

They forgot the driver!

So they went to look for him.
They looked in the park.

They looked in the street.
They looked and they called.

At last they found him.

The driver was
so happy
to see them.

His horse was
so happy
to see him.

"You are a very good driver,"
he said to Grandma.

"Thank you," said Grandma,
"Would you like us to give you
a ride?

"I would," said the driver.

So they did.